CITY KIDS

Ann and Robb eagerly anticipate the unusual vacation with their ranger-uncle Jack Lewis and his wife, but never in their wildest dreams did they imagine they'd play starring roles in the drama that was to unfold in those forests of the Pacific Northwest.

Eagerly they agree to act as lookouts. Too soon they see one fire . . . and then another . . . and then the empty kerosene cans that spell arson! And before they realize what has happened, Ann and Robb find themselves in a life-or-death situation where prayer is their only hope!

FIRE!

Anita Deyneka

Illustrated by
Seymour Fleishman

David C. Cook Publishing Co.
ELGIN, ILLINOIS—WESTON, ONTARIO

Dedicated to my brothers—
Lee, David, Allan, and Dean

CONTENTS

1 City Slickers

"Lightning!" Ranger Jack Lewis frowned. "Look at that sky glow above Alpine Mountain. If lightning strikes that ridge, the whole forest is likely to turn into a huge bonfire!"

Jack Lewis studied the distant mountain grimly. Eerie streaks of lightning danced in the sky on top of the ridge. Suddenly the sky turned an angry gray. A distant rumble of thunder boomed from beyond Alpine Mountain.

Jack Lewis' 10-year-old niece, Ann, watched the lightning zigzag crazy patterns across the sky. Alpine Mountain was a long way from her Uncle Jack's solid green ranger station house set on the shore of Lake Wenatchee, but Ann tensed as the gloom of the storm crept closer. She edged close to her brother Robb who stood absorbed in the excitement of the fireworks lighting the horizon.

Ann's apprehension grew as she saw her Uncle Jack stare grimly at the mountain. To everybody else around the forest service compound, Uncle Jack was the ranger—admired and respected for his responsibility as chief supervisor of the vast Lake Wenatchee forest district.

To Ann, he was Uncle Jack—her father's brother whom she had never really known before this summer. The only times she could remember Uncle Jack and his wife, Aunt Betty, were twice when they had come on short trips to Chicago. Then they had always been in a hurry to return to their forest.

"Well, 380,000 square acres is a big responsibility," Ann's father had told her once when she had asked about her uncle's work. "Your Uncle Jack has walked over almost every section of the Lake Wenatchee forest. He knows the land like a map." Ann looked up at her tall uncle and felt reassured. The ranger seemed strong enough to stride up any mountain.

Uncle Jack glanced anxiously from the lightning to his watch. He counted the seconds out loud between the lightning bolts and the thunder that roared heavily after the streaks stabbing through the sky.

A flashing bolt of lightning lit the ridge. Almost simultaneously the thud of thunder shook the house. "That was close!" Uncle Jack glanced at his watch again. "In the mountains we worry when thunder follows the lightning that soon."

"When the lightning comes close to the mountain—does that mean it struck timber?" The storm was so beautiful that Robb hadn't thought to worry before.

"We don't know for sure until the forester in the mountain lookout or the pilot in the fire detection plane spots the fire," Uncle Jack replied soberly. "Sometimes the lightning just knocks off a tree top without starting a fire. And sometimes . . . even in lightning as close as that one . . ." a roar of thunder interrupted the ranger's words. "Sometimes if we're lucky the lightning doesn't hit anything," Uncle Jack shouted over the thunder growling in the distance.

"But this season I don't think we are going to be so lucky . . ." a troubled expression flickered across the ranger's face. "This year the forest is as dry as a tinder box—almost no rain and a lot of wind."

"Is that why the needle on the big chart by the ranger station is pointing to red?" Robb's eyes widened.

"That's right—extreme fire danger," the ranger replied grimly. "If a lightning bolt did strike anywhere on the Lake Wenatchee forest now, it would be like one gigantic match setting fire to kindling wood!

"Between the lightning and careless tourists, I'm glad you two are here to help put out the fires this summer," Uncle Jack spoke in his deep voice. He turned from the storm for the first time and smiled at his niece and nephew.

Uncle Jack's wife, Aunt Betty, who preferred working to almost every other activity, wiped her hands on her apron as she walked briskly from the kitchen into the big living room, where a wide window looked out over the lake toward Alpine Mountain.

"Watching the storm doesn't make it disappear," she remarked sensibly as she settled herself stiffly on the couch and reached for her knitting bag. She picked out a gray woolen sweater she was knitting.

Her knitting needles clicked rapidly. "It's a good thing your father's company sent your parents on a business trip to Japan this summer. Otherwise we might never have had a chance to show you city children our mountain country. From the way the sky looks tonight, you two will see plenty of action before this summer is over!"

As if the performance were over for the night, the lightning slipped back into the folds of the dusky sky. "Well, that's it. But I don't hear any rain yet. That thirsty forest needs buckets of rain," Uncle Jack sighed.

Mountain air cooled by the storm fluttered the starched white curtains at Ann's bedroom window. Ann breathed deeply and snuggled the warm quilt around her chin. Gradually, she heard the caress of rain on the shingled roof and wondered if Uncle Jack were still awake listening.

Thunderstorms were nothing new to Ann —all her life in Chicago she could remember ferocious storms that shook the house on the elm-shaded street where she lived. But the towering mountains, graceful pine trees, and orange tiger lilies that clung to the mountain slopes in Washington State were new—a wild contrast from the flat countryside and noisy streets Ann had known.

That night Aunt Betty had called her and Robb "city children." It was true, Ann thought. She had never been far away from

Chicago before. Now she and Robb were at Lake Wenatchee for the whole summer . . . away from their parents . . . away from their friends . . . in the mountains that had seemed full of mystery to Ann as they drove from the airport in Seattle along the winding road up Stevens Pass.

Ann pulled the quilt that her aunt had called a "comforter" closer. She wasn't exactly afraid of the mountains whose peaks probed the sky, she decided, but still she felt uneasy . . . worried that other people at Lake Wenatchee might call her a "city child" as if she and Robb didn't belong.

Ann didn't like the feeling that she didn't fit. It was her freckles spread solid like a mask across her face, she reflected, that usually made her feel a misfit. Ruefully, Ann touched her cheek as if she could rub out the sunny spots sprinkled thickly across her nose. But every day under the summer sun, Ann had felt new freckles coming.

Ann remembered the night before she and Robb left Chicago. "I hope you have lots more pretty freckles by the time you come back to Chicago, Annie," her father had said.

Ann's thoughts took her back to that last night in Chicago. Her family had read the Bible and prayed together as always.

Her father read from the Old Testament about the Syrian captain Naaman and the Israeli servant girl who told the captain about God. "Uncle Jack and Aunt Betty aren't Christians," Ann's father had said. "Maybe that's why God is sending you two to stay with Aunt Betty and Uncle Jack this summer.

"Uncle Jack and I used to go to Sunday school together when we were boys growing up in Montana," Ann's father remembered back to his childhood. "But then Uncle Jack went to forestry school and his work became everything to him. Somehow, he didn't have time for God anymore."

"Uncle Jack must have forgotten that God created the forest," Ann said sadly.

Ann climbed out of the warm covers and knelt beside her bed. "Please, God . . . help Robb and me to know how to tell Uncle Jack and Aunt Betty about You." Ann thought of the frightening storm. "And please, Lord, protect the forest."

By morning the rain had stopped and Ann felt the warm sun through the window rousing her. She pulled back the curtains to welcome the new day and Lake Wenatchee resting without a ripple.

Suddenly out of the stillness, Ann saw a flicker of movement in the maple bushes beside the lake. Curious, she leaned out the open bedroom window.

A freckled fawn nosed its way out of the leaves. Cautiously the little animal teetered toward the deep lake.

Ann wished she could reach from the window and guide the fawn safely away from the water.

Stealthily she crept out on the porch bordering her bedroom—her eyes fixed on the fawn who seemed as dewy as the morning. She longed to reach out to the little animal.

In her nightgown, Ann slipped softly down the steps of the wooden porch toward the shore of the lake.

The fawn reached the lake and thirstily drank the clear water. Then he turned from the lake to the bushes where Ann waited.

But the little animal didn't dart away. The fawn stood like a statue and studied the slender girl in the long nightgown.

"Breakfast . . . breakfast! Where are you?" Robb's echoing shout broke the stillness and the startled fawn sprinted away through the forest.

"Oh, Robb! You scared my fawn. Did you see him?" Ann stumbled in her long nightgown up the mountain. "He was so beautiful. Maybe he would have come to me."

At breakfast Ann told Aunt Betty about

the fawn. "That little fawn is one reason your Uncle Jack cares so much about the forest," Aunt Betty said sternly. "One careless camper can thoughtlessly start a fire that will burn that fawn—and thousands of helpless animals—out of their homes."

"Do the animals ever die in the fire?" Ann felt a choking in her throat.

"Sometimes—if the fire traps them in the forest," Aunt Betty answered shortly.

"Uncle Jack is already up at the ranger station," Aunt Betty explained as she piled blackberry pancakes onto a platter. "After you two finish eating, why don't you hike up the hill to the station? Uncle Jack might show you the forest service compound."

Aunt Betty dropped another spoonful of batter in the frying pan and sprinkled blackberries across the top. She motioned up the hill with her other hand. "Go across the road past the big warehouse, past the crew bunkhouse to the green building with the American flag in front. That's the main station. Uncle Jack will be working in his office.

"If you hurry you can catch him before he goes out to the woods—in fact he'll probably ask you to ride along," she said, briskly dropping another pancake on Robb's plate.

"Hurry, Ann!" Excited, Robb led the way at a trot up the slope to the station. The compound which had seemed so quiet the night before stirred with activity.

Foresters in green uniforms and orange metal hats hurried to work. Some of the men carried briefcases and walked toward the ranger station office. Others drove away from the compound in vehicles loaded with axes, shovels, and other equipment ready for work in the woods. One brown pack horse stood watching the excitement and chewing alfalfa hay, while an old man strapped heavy packs on the horse's back.

At first glance, all the men in their green uniforms looked the same. Then Ann noticed several boys coming up the hill from the bunkhouse. They looked older than Robb and they wore forest service uniforms. Ann wished her freckles would fade away.

"So you two city slickers decided to get up, did you?" Uncle Jack pretended to sound gruff. "Come on. Let me introduce you," he said with an arm around each of them. "It's not every day we have a niece and nephew visiting from Chicago.

"But the tour is going to be a swift one. I have to head out to the woods and check a new reforestation project—a patch of ground where the foresters are replanting trees," the ranger paused to explain when he noticed Ann's perplexed expression.

Covering three steps at a time, the ranger led the way up the stairs and down the hall.

He pushed open the door into a big office. "Here's the timber department. The foresters here supervise loggers who cut trees for lumber. They also plant new trees."

Uncle Jack led the children into a room with high tables cluttered with compasses, triangles and rulers. "This looks like math class," Robb exclaimed.

"A good guess," Uncle Jack replied. "The engineers who work here do use arithmetic —to build roads through the forest.

"And here," Uncle Jack swung wide the door to a large room filled with huge maps and a big radio, "is what we call 'fire control' in the forest service."

The ranger lowered his voice. "The fire control chief is talking on the two-way radio to one of the mountain lookouts."

The fire chief spoke slowly into the radio phone, "960—this is central ranger station calling Dirtyface lookout station. How does the weather look up on Dirtyface Mountain today? How did you survive that storm?"

The guard's voice crackled back over the receiver. "That was a wild one! The tower on my lookout house shook, but I sat on the lightning stool the whole time. If the lightning did strike the peak of Dirtyface Mountain, I knew I would at least be grounded to the stool since it doesn't conduct electricity.

"But I'm worried." Even over the radio Ann heard the apprehension in the guard's voice. "If that lightning struck dry ground cover on the forest below me—we're going to have trouble. I just hope we don't have any sleepers," the guard warned.

"Sleepers—what are sleepers?" Ann whispered anxiously to her uncle.

"That's forest service talk," Uncle Jack grinned. "Sometimes the lightning storm ignites fires which don't spread until a few days after the storm—they're sleepers."

"Robb," Ann nudged her brother, "I'm scared. Uncle Jack is worried, the mountain lookout guard is afraid—what's going to happen this summer? And Robb—if there's a fire, what will happen to my fawn?"

"He's not your fawn," Robb whispered.

"Well, keep a sharp eye on your territory," the fire chief instructed the mountain guard, whose name was Bruce, over the radio phone. "In ten minutes use your instruments to make a complete check of the forest. Call me back if you see anything even slightly suspicious."

The fire chief hung up the radio phone and turned to the children. He gestured to a huge map spread on the wall before him.

"We have plenty of lakes and rivers in this district," he explained, "but this year we didn't get enough snow. And we have had gales of wind. That combination dried out the forest.

"If a fire does start, it will burn wild. Trees . . . animals . . . maybe even people," the chief said soberly. "If fire starts now, it could wipe out everything in its path."

In minutes, Ann recognized the mountain guard's voice again booming over the two-way radio. "4-11! Fire! 4-11! Fire!" The guard shouted so loudly it seemed almost as if the radio might jump off the wall. Instantly, Uncle Jack was at the radio beside the fire chief. The men's faces were tense.

"4-11! Fire!" the guard shouted again. "T 28 north, section 18 . . ." carefully the lookout located the fire. "It's up Chiwawa River Road!"

"Radio the location to the fire retardant plane immediately," the chief ordered the lookout. "I'll dispatch fire fighters up to the blaze right away." The chief grabbed his metal hat and turned toward the door.

The mountain lookout's voice tensed urgently over the radio. "I can't figure out how this fire started so fast. Smoke is billowing out like a bomb!"

2 George's Close Call

"Quick! Follow me," Uncle Jack commanded. Half running, he led the children down the hill. "I'll grab my pack from the warehouse. You climb in," he motioned to the light green pickup with the forest service emblem emblazoned on the side.

As Ann climbed the high step into the pickup, she glimpsed her aunt running breathlessly up the hill from the ranger house. "I heard about the fire on the two-way radio in our kitchen," Aunt Betty panted.

She shoved a lunch basket on the seat next to them. "In case that fire turns out to be a long one, you'll be hungry. It's a good thing you two wore your old clothes today, but you're both a bit young to be fighting fires," she fussed. "They'd better stay in the pickup, Jack," she addressed her husband with a look of concern.

"Don't worry, Betty. They'll be safe—.they're going with the ranger, remember," and he smiled at his anxious wife. "I'll be in touch with you over the radio if we're delayed past dark," Uncle Jack promised his wife as he swung into the pickup.

Lake Wenatchee rolled in the wind as the ranger swiftly steered the pickup along the straight paved highway which bordered its banks. The ranger glanced anxiously at the wind-tossed waves. "That breeze will fan those flames like a dinosaur breath if we don't stop that fire soon," he worried.

After several miles, the road veered from the glittering lake through woods and open fields. Then the road swerved sharply to the left. A rustic wood sign, "Chiwawa River Road," marked the turn.

"Chiwawa means 'sparkling water,' " Uncle Jack explained. "It's an Indian name like Wenatchee and a lot of other names of places in this district."

The pickup bumped over the rutted dirt road. "Now you're on a forest service road,"

Uncle Jack said.

"It's—it's not exactly like an Illinois toll-way . . ." Robb searched for a way to describe the scenic road through the forest.

"We're not trying to turn the forest into a city with asphalt roads," Uncle Jack chuckled, "but we do figure it's important that people have access into the mountains —just to enjoy the beauty of them."

The ranger swerved the pickup to avoid hitting a chipmunk that scurried across the road. "If it weren't for these dirt roads which reach all over the forest, we'd really be in a fix when it comes to fighting fires. Years ago, it used to take days to even reach the fire—by that time thousands of acres were already ruined.

"And in those days," Uncle Jack added, "there were no planes to parachute men in to fight the fire. There were no planes to fly over the fire and drop chemical retardant to smother the flames."

The ranger skillfully maneuvered the pickup around the winding roads. Waves of dust churned past the windows, coating Ann's long, sandy hair, but she didn't complain. Instead, she wished she were sitting closer to the intriguing forest whizzing by.

Chiwawa River Road climbed sharply along a towering cliff. Ann turned her eyes from the side of the narrow road which plunged steeply to the river below. "I hope Old George has unchained that gate across Chiwawa Road," the ranger muttered, never taking his eyes from the winding road.

"Who's Old George?" Ann wanted to ask, but she saw her uncle's preoccupied expression and decided to wait. In moments Ann spied rusty spirals of smoke ahead and knew they were approaching the fire.

Uncle Jack surveyed the scene ahead as he drove. "The fire is still a ways in the distance yet, but the wind is blowing it this way fast. We have to build a firebreak in front of the fire. That way we hope to stop it before it ever reaches the foot of this hill. We'll keep pushing the fire back into the Chiwawa River until we drown it."

The ranger skidded the pickup to a stop on top of a plateau overlooking the fire. Foresters from the ranger station who had followed in the caravan behind Uncle Jack's pickup scrambled down the sloping ridge to the fire.

Robb looked wistfully at the forest service crew, and Ann knew he wanted to climb down to the fire too. But Aunt Betty had said they shouldn't even get out of the pickup. "I wish I were older," Robb groaned softly.

The ranger glanced from a menacing gust of smoke he had been watching rise from the valley below. He put a quick arm around his nephew's shoulder. "Do you think you can stay at the edge of the clearing in front of the fire?" Robb nodded emphatically. "Well, then I think you're old enough to go down the ravine with me and fight fire!"

"But Ann," her uncle added quickly, "you'd better stay up here on the hill. You can go as far as the edge of the bluff. You'll get a good view of what's happening below —and most of all you'll be safe. Here," the ranger jerked a pair of binoculars from his pack, "you can see everything through these."

"Come on, Robb," the ranger said briskly, "every minute counts." Uncle Jack lifted two shovels from the pickup into Robb's hands. The ranger shouldered the heavy pack himself that he had loaded from the warehouse. "Take good care of that lunch, Ann," Uncle Jack hollered back. "We'll be hungry as horses by the time we get this one under control!"

Momentarily, Ann wished she could coil her long brown hair up under a forest service tin hat, wear a green uniform, and climb down the ravine with the men. "Well, at least Robb got to go," she grumbled to herself. Then she thought of Robb's sparkling eyes when Uncle Jack said he could "fight fire," and she was glad for him.

Ann hurried to the edge of the bluff and looked down into the valley. From the distance below she heard popping, crackling sounds of fire as the greedy flames gobbled pine needles, underbrush, and even trees. She fumbled with the binoculars and finally the scene below came into focus as if the fire were only a few yards away. In fascination, she watched the panorama.

Powerful yellow bulldozers cleared a path ahead of the fire that resembled a wide belt. Men with chain saws and axes were felling shaggy trees to clear the firebreak. Shovelsful of dirt flew into the air as the foresters cleared the ground to bare earth to halt the fire.

Besides the forest service crew, easily identifiable by their green uniforms, there were several other men driving bulldozers or cutting trees. They must be the loggers, Ann decided. She had heard her uncle say that loggers working in the nearby woods would come to help fight the fire.

She followed the men with the binoculars through the hazy smoke as they struggled to clear a dirt strip where the fire could burn itself out. The men worked fast, but menacing gusts of smoke from the fire behind billowed bigger and closer. Puffs of gray smoke strayed toward Ann and stung her eyes.

Suddenly Ann heard a whirring sound overhead. She lifted her eyes and saw a plane swoop daringly low over the fire. The plane left a burst of red, blotchy retardant spray in its trail. Globs of red retardant clung to the trees and spattered on the ground. The smoke seemed to subside.

From the hill through her binoculars, Ann spotted Uncle Jack and Robb in the ravine below. The ranger, his shovel in his hand, moved from crew to crew giving orders.

One of the foresters in a green uniform dug his power saw blade into a tall tree on a slope above him. Like a clumsy giant, the tree started to wobble. But the forester went on cutting.

Ann gasped. Fear strangled her and she wanted to scream, "Run!" but she knew her voice would never be heard above the whine of the saws and the noisy bulldozers. "Help that man, Lord!" she prayed.

By the time the forester realized his danger, the tree was toppling toward him. The forester, his chain saw in his hand, stood bewildered—transfixed beneath the thundering giant.

Suddenly a boy working beside the forester lunged toward the frightened man. The tree thudded to the ground as the forester and the boy rolled to safety only inches away from the crushing tree.

Trembling, Ann dropped her binoculars and slumped back to the ravine. "Thank You, God," she whispered. "Thank You for saving their lives."

Ann watched as Uncle Jack and some of the other men crowded around the fallen tree. Seemingly unscathed, the frightened forester and the boy lifted themselves from the ground.

Uncle Jack retrieved the mangled saw from under the tree's limp branches. He handed an ax to the shaken forester, who listlessly began to trim limbs from the fallen tree.

The muscular, tawny boy who had rescued the forester looked younger than most of the firefighters—but a little older than Robb. Ann noticed the boy didn't wear a forest service uniform. "He must be a logger," she decided. The boy picked up an ax and agilely helped the forester limb the tree. Ann watched the boy through her binoculars.

Several minutes later, Ann heard her uncle's heavy footsteps crunch toward the pickup. The ranger was streaked with sweat and smoke. He carried a water canteen in his hands.

"Oh, Uncle Jack," Ann shuddered, "that man was almost killed! What happened?"

"So you saw the narrow escape, did you?" Uncle Jack replied grimly. "That crazy forester George Olson could have killed himself. He must have slept through all the safety courses!

"The forester tried to cut the tree from the downhill side," the ranger explained. "He expected the tree to fall the opposite direction—not on him. If it hadn't been for that fast-thinking logger's kid, Brian Madson, forester George Olson would have been dead!"

Ann kept pace with her uncle's rapid steps to the pickup. She held the canteen as he refilled it with water for the thirsty fire fighters below. "With luck we'll have a good start on that fire within another hour, and a new crew will come to replace us for the night. But this fire is a mean one," the ranger wiped sweat and dust from his face. "Probably some careless camper started the whole thing," he observed crossly as he strode back toward the fire.

Ann settled herself again on the forest bench overlooking the fire. Sadly she thought of the forest the fire was devouring in its path. She thought of the timid fawn she had seen that morning on the shore of Lake Wenatchee. She was glad he was far from the fire. "But the other animals who live down in the ravine! What will happen to them?" she worried.

Suddenly Ann heard a rustling sound in the maple bushes behind her. "Maybe it is a fawn fleeing from the fire," she thought sadly. Silently she tiptoed toward the bushes.

She peeked through the branches and gasped. A man with a shotgun slung across his back was staring at the fire in the ravine below.

The man heard Ann gasp. He glanced at her for a second and slunk off.

Frightened, Ann crept back toward her uncle's pickup. A forest service truck chugged to a stop behind her and a new crew of fire fighters climbed out the back. Slowly the exhausted fire fighters, black and sooty, straggled up the hill from the fire below as the new foresters hurried down to replace them.

Ann ran to meet her uncle climbing wearily up the hill. "Uncle Jack," she panted. "Just a few minutes ago—I saw a man in the bushes . . . he had a gun over his shoulder. I just saw his face for a second, but he looked scary!"

"Hm . . . that's strange, but maybe the man was just hunting squirrels and stopped to see the fire. He probably meant no harm," the ranger dismissed Ann's anxiety.

Uncle Jack gulped a last drink of water from the canteen. While the ranger still held the canteen to his lips, Robb ran anxiously up the hill toward his uncle. "Uncle Jack, look! Look what I found around the back side of the fire," and Robb held up two cans. Both cans said, "BOGGS KEROSENE" in large letters across the front.

"Uncle Jack," Robb clutched the kerosene cans tensely, "you said a careless camper caused the fire—but what about these kerosene cans? Do you think somebody set the fire on purpose?"

Uncle Jack's face, already haggard, grew even grimmer. "I'm afraid you might be right, Robb," he said soberly.

"I figured the fire must have been caused by a careless camper because I found no evidence that a lightning strike had started it. Now, it looks like the fire might have been set on purpose—by an arsonist!

"But why," Uncle Jack mused, "would an arsonist leave the evidence—the kerosene cans—at the site of the fire?"

3 Mulling Over the Clues

The next day Uncle Jack and Robb drove back up Chiwawa River Road to check the fire. Ann volunteered to help her aunt pick blackberries on the high mountain behind the ranger station.

Eagerly, Ann lifted the blackberry vine. She popped one of the hard green berries into her mouth, but she made a face at the sour taste and spit the berry on the ground.

"Only the plump purple berries are ripe, Ann," Aunt Betty bent into the thick vines. "Of course you probably never saw a blackberry vine in the city."

Ann hadn't seen a blackberry vine. In the city, she had also never stood on such a high mountain. "You have to drive high to find the best berries," Aunt Betty had insisted.

Ann settled herself back on the slope of the steep mountain and savored the view spread before her. Lake Wenatchee far below seemed small. The peak of Alpine Mountain on the opposite side of the lake lay almost straight across from her.

Ann twisted back lazily against the warm ground. A thistly branch pricked her elbow. She moved aside, her thoughts turning to the fire of three days before. "Aunt Betty, why would anybody set fire to anything so beautiful—to the forest?"

Aunt Betty didn't pause from her berry-picking, and Ann wondered if her aunt ever stopped to sample the berries she picked. "Most fires aren't set on purpose," Aunt Betty swiftly dropped a handful of berries in the bucket. "Most are set by careless people—or by lightning. But now and again arsonists come into the forest—criminals who start fires on purpose," she straightened her shoulders disapprovingly.

"It's probably summer people who set the fire," she observed grumpily, "—that rabble from the city. You can be sure none of us old timers would set fire to our forest!"

Even in the short time she and Robb had been at Lake Wenatchee, Ann had heard her aunt speak often of "old timers." She understood that her aunt meant the people who lived in the area all year 'round—like the foresters, farmers, and loggers.

Ann knew there were other people who came only for the summer. Hundreds of summer cottages dotted the shores of Lake Wenatchee. Besides the summer people there were thousands of tourists who swarmed to the lake for a few days vacation.

With a shudder Ann suddenly remembered the man she had glimpsed the day of the fire—sneaking through the bushes. She had only seen him for a second, but he looked like an "old timer." But maybe, as Uncle Jack had said, the man was just shooting squirrels . . . just curious to see the fire . . . maybe he wasn't the arsonist at all.

Ann thought about the arsonist. How could anyone purposely destroy acres of beautiful towering forest . . . the home of helpless animals . . . forest which her uncle worked so hard to protect . . . forest that God had created?

"Maybe the arsonist will start more fires," Ann agonized aloud. "Please, God," she prayed, "help Uncle Jack find the arsonist before he sets more fires . . . before he hurts the forest again."

Back at the ranger house, Aunt Betty gently washed the tender blackberries and laid most of them in a plastic container. "We'll freeze those for a pie later," she explained. She poured the rest in a big bowl that she set on the table with a pitcher of milk and a dish of honey.

"Ranger Lewis to ranger residence . . ." the radio phone on the wall crackled and Ann jumped. She still found the forest service radio that bristled unexpectedly with talk of the forest a startling interruption.

"Betty," Ann heard her uncle's voice over the radio, "Robb and I are on our way home from checking the fire. We'll be home in ten minutes . . ."

Ann heard the crunch of her uncle's pickup in the driveway. "Is the fire out?" she rushed to greet her uncle and Robb.

"Yup . . . even the last smoldering stumps look like they won't give us any more trouble," the ranger smiled.

"But Uncle Jack has foresters stationed at the fire to be sure the fire doesn't start—or that somebody doesn't start it again," Robb added importantly.

"I'm going to investigate that fire," Uncle Jack said with determination when they had eaten lunch. "You two want to go with me?"

He scraped his chair away from the table and looked toward the children.

The ranger guided the pickup down the North Shore Road that ran alongside Lake Wenatchee—the same route the children had followed with their uncle the day of the fire.

"Uncle Jack," Ann's voice was eager, "maybe Robb and I can help you solve the mystery of the arsonist fire. This morning up on the mountain picking blackberries," her voice faltered, "I—I prayed God would protect the forest . . . and help you find the arsonist."

"Well—I guess I won't turn down the help of two praying detectives," the ranger smiled at his niece and nephew.

At the turnoff to Chiwawa Road, a grizzled old man, with a battered cowboy hat and leather boots, strapped packs on two horses who stood patiently in the hot sun flicking mosquitoes with their long tails.

Uncle Jack waved hello to the old man. "That's Cleo the forest service packer," he said. Turning back to look out the pickup window, Ann gazed at the old cowboy who wore a rumpled green forest service uniform.

"The packer is loading the horses to haul food supplies into one of the lookout stations," the ranger explained.

"I guess the horses are the only ones strong enough to carry the heavy supplies up the mountain trail," Robb mused aloud.

"For a city boy, you've got a lot of country sense," the ranger smiled at his nephew, and Robb flushed happily at his uncle's compliment.

"We're going to drive up past the fire all the way to the end of Chiwawa River Road to Red Mountain Mine," Uncle Jack outlined his plan for the afternoon. "Then we three detectives are going to start hunting for clues at Red Mountain Mine and work our way back down Chiwawa River Road."

"Is it a real mine, Uncle Jack? Will we see the miners hauling gold out of the mountain?" Robb's questions erupted excitedly.

Uncle Jack smiled, "I'm afraid Red Mountain Mine is what we call a ghost mine. Red Mountain Mine used to be one of the richest gold mines in the Pacific Northwest," the ranger explained, "but it hasn't operated for forty years. Now it's nothing but a bunch of tumbledown buildings and some old mining shafts ready to cave in."

"Did prospectors really mine gold from Red Mountain?" Ann's eyes sparkled with excitement.

"In boom days, people came all the way

from the East—hoping to find gold nuggets and strike it rich. Very few found gold. But after they lived in the mountains, many of the miners didn't want to go home. Some of them staked land or homesteaded. Others logged or worked for the railroad."

"Does anybody live at Red Mountain Mine now?" Robb asked. Before the ranger could reply, he jerked the pickup to a stop. A padlocked gate barred the road.

Etched crudely on the sign was the warning, "STAY OUT! ALL TRESPASSERS WILL BE SHOT ON SIGHT."

4 Meeting with a Cranky Old Timer

Ann stared at the threatening sign looming before them. "Please, Uncle Jack, let's not try to go any farther," she gripped her uncle's arm. Her own arm shook with fear.

Ann trembled as she imagined a man who might be lurking in the bushes on the mountain—his gun loaded, ready to snipe trespassers. In her terror, it seemed to Ann she could almost hear bullets pounding the pickup.

"Uncle Jack, can't you back the pickup down the road or just turn around here?" she pleaded. Even Robb, who usually tried to at least look brave, sat silent and shaken.

"Are we going to turn around, Uncle Jack?" his voice quavered. "Are we?"

The ranger reached a reassuring arm around his niece trembling on the seat beside him. "You know what I was saying about a few old miners who stayed on— well, you're about to meet one of them.

"You don't need to be afraid. That's how Old George wants people to react when they see his sign, but there's really nothing to fear. His bark is worse than his bite.

"Old George staked a mining claim here fifty years ago. The law says that as long as he does a little work each year on his piece of land, he has a right to keep the claim. But that's only about two acres. All the rest of this land is public property . . . Old George just tries to frighten people away with his sign."

"I'll bet he succeeds a lot of the time!" Robb exclaimed. "Boy, Ann sure was scared!" he observed bravely, forgetting how frightened he had been himself.

"Old George is a hard man to figure out," Uncle Jack admitted. "And what is worse, he seems to be getting more eccentric all the time. Lately, he's even been angry with me when I have to drive past his gate."

Ann felt apprehension creeping back. "Are you sure we have to go through his gate, Uncle Jack?"

The ranger jiggled the padlock. "Yup, it's locked all right," he said. He strode back to the pickup and honked the horn.

The bushes crackled and an old man with a shotgun slung across his shoulder moved slowly toward the car. Ann huddled close to her uncle.

"Ya can quit your honkin'—I heard ya—I'm comin'," the old man snarled. Ann stared at the old miner with the strange sensation that she had seen him somewhere before. His neck was red and wrinkled. A frown seemed frozen on his face. His eyes, lost in folds of skin, scowled.

"Hi, George . . . thanks for opening the gate," Uncle Jack ignored the old man's grumpy greeting with a smile. The miner shrugged one shoulder in reply and un- locked the gate, which creaked open reluc- tantly.

"Well, drive on through so I ken lock her up agin," Old George jerked his hand at the gate. "I guess yu'll have to honk on yer way out if ya wanna git through agin."

The ranger rested his elbow on the gate, "Well—I'm not driving on to Red Mountain Mine—not just yet anyway, George. I want to visit with you a few minutes."

"Visit with me," the old miner gaped suspiciously, "I ain't had visitors for twenty years. All I git are trespassers. I s'pose yer visit has somethin' to do with that fire the other day." Old George shifted uneasily, "Well, I don't know nuthin'."

"Did you let anybody through your gate the day of the fire or the day before?" Uncle Jack asked. "Did you notice anybody at all around here?"

"Oh, so yah suspect somebody set the fire, do yuh," Old George evaded the ranger's question. "How should I know who's comin' and goin', Ranger? I'm busy workin' muh claim. All's I know is that everything was peaceful and quiet 'til the day of the fire when yer fire fightin' crew made me take muh gate down."

"Well," the ranger's voice grew sterner, "since you keep your gate padlocked, George, it is likely you would see anybody who drove through. And since your cabin is by the gate, it is reasonable you would have seen anybody who came near the fire area," Uncle Jack stared straight into the old man's eyes.

"What ya implyin', Ranger?" a sly expression flickered across Old George's inscrutable face and Ann felt frightened. "How'd I know who set the fire . . . next thing yuh'll be suspectin' me I s'pose!"

The old man snorted, "It's not us old timers—it's the newcomers that's ruinin' this here land. If it wuz only like the good old days," he grumbled.

"It's yer fault if somebody started that fire," Old George suddenly accused the ranger. Defensively, Ann moved closer to her uncle as the old man raged, "If yuh didn't make me take down my gate to let strangers through, I guarantee there wouldn't be no trouble. Can I help it the crazy critters that are wanderin' around here now since yah told me I have to take down the gate cuz the forest's publik property!"

"Did you see anyone in the fire area?" the ranger quietly ignored the old man's tantrum.

Old George scratched his head, "There's that arkeologist or sumthing he calls hisself. He's been slinkin' around these here woods all summer. I'd like to shoot the stupid coyote," Old George fingered his rifle. But as much as Ann feared the old miner, she sensed he didn't really mean his gruff words.

Patiently the ranger tried again. "So there's the archaeologist and the tourists. Think hard, George. Was there anybody else through those two days?"

"Yuh think I just set here all day a-look-ing?" the old man grumped. "Why don't yuh ask that young whippersnapper yuh got workin' for you at the guard station up the road? Maybe he ken tell yuh who comes up Chiwawa River Road—that is if he ain't too busy swimming in the Chiwawa River," and the old man chuckled to himself.

"Well, I gotta git back to work, Ranger. Maybe you governmint people don't have nothin' else to do but sit and visit, but I gotta git back to work," Old George repeated as he shuffled heavily down the road.

Uncle Jack headed the pickup past the gate and up the road toward Red Mountain Mine. "Well, you've met Old George," he said.

Ann wrinkled her nose. She had not liked the old man. But suddenly she grasped her uncle's arm. "Old George! He looked so familiar!" she exclaimed excitedly. "I knew I had seen him somewhere. I—I think he's the one I saw sneaking through the bushes the day of the fire!"

"Hmm," the ranger pondered his niece's words, "it might have been Old George all right. That does look suspicious," Uncle Jack admitted, "but on the other hand, the old man might have just come down to check what was happening at the fire and didn't want anybody to see him."

"Well, he gives me the creeps," Ann shuddered. "He is an awful old man and I wouldn't be surprised if he did set the fire himself!"

Her uncle looked at her strangely. "You're not the only one who's going to be saying that, Ann. A lot of people around Lake Wenatchee haven't trusted Old George for a long time. He's grumpy to everybody and he sticks by himself. But just because he's different doesn't mean that he is guilty."

"That's right," Robb chimed in helpfully. "How would you like it, Ann, if people said you were different just because you had— well, so many freckles for example," he teased his sister.

"Robb Lewis!" Ann shoved her brother sharply with her elbow. "That's just mean. You know I can't help my . . . freckles," she muttered the hated word.

"What's Old George's real name, Uncle Jack?" Robb ignored his sulking sister.

"Nobody knows for sure. That's why they call him Old George. He came here as a young man during one of the mining booms." Uncle Jack steered the pickup slowly up the rutted road. "Old George caught the hankering for gold and just stayed on. He never discovered any gold, but he did stake out two acres. He's often vowed that nothing or nobody would make him move—and I guess he's right.

"Ever since I've known Old George, he's always wanted to be by himself and keep others out of the area around his claim. He has a shack—that one you saw by the gate. I believe he might shoot—at least in the air as a warning—if somebody tried to come inside his shack. He's not what you'd call hospitable.

"Old George hasn't had a very happy life," Uncle Jack kept his eyes on the road as he continued his story. "The old timers here say that he married a young school teacher who taught in the one-room school up at the mining camp. They had one son.

"One winter day Old George's wife was alone in the cabin. The miner had taken his little boy outside. A snow avalanche came down and buried the cabin. By the time Old George reached his wife, she was dead.

"Folks say Old George was never quite the same after that. He built another cabin —exactly like the one destroyed in the avalanche and I guess he tried to raise his son.

"But something happened between him and his son. The boy ran away from home when he was 10 years old and folks around here say that Old George hasn't seen or heard of his son since."

While he was telling Old George's story, Uncle Jack reached the end of Chiwawa Road. The ranger and the children sat silent in the pickup when he had finished.

"I wonder if Old George has a Bible?" Robb spoke through the silence. "Even if Old George doesn't have any friends—God still cares about him. I—I wish I could give him a Bible," Robb said impulsively.

Uncle Jack said nothing, but Ann felt sorry. She had never stopped to consider that the cranky old man might be lonely. She didn't like his crabby face or mean talk, but Robb was right. Old George needed God for his friend, too.

"There's only one thing more that bothers me about Old George," Uncle Jack hesitated before he stepped out of the pickup. "There was a kerosene can on the porch of his cabin. The can said, 'BOGGS KEROSENE,'" the ranger paused heavily.

"Of course, just because the miner uses the same brand of kerosene as the cans we found at the fire doesn't mean he's guilty. Still, it does look suspicious," Uncle Jack struggled with the mystery.

5 Suspicious Bungling

"This is as far as the road goes," the ranger said when the children climbed out of the pickup. From here we will hike the next quarter mile by trail up to the mine."

From a distance Ann saw the ramshackle mine buildings fading into the forest.

"Well, there you have Red Mountain Mine—or at least a ghost of what it used to be," Uncle Jack gestured ahead to the crumbled buildings and caved shafts huddled forlorn and lonely against the majestic mountain. With difficulty Ann tried to picture the days when Red Mountain Mine had been a "boom town."

The Red Mountain Mine forest service lookout station stood on a clearing three bends in the trail past the mine. Two tall pines framed the neat rustic cabin. A forest service sign, "Red Mountain Lookout Station—For tourist information inquire here—George Olson, guard," hung crookedly from one of the trees.

"Isn't he the one who almost killed himself when he cut the tree wrong at the Chiwawa fire?" Ann recognized Olson's name.

"That's right," the ranger said grimly.

Uncle Jack paused to straighten the sign and knocked on the cabin door. "Oh, Ranger Lewis," said forest service guard George Olson, nervously putting down the teakettle he held in his hand. "Er . . . come in, sir. I was just preparing a cup of tea . . . would you all," he glanced at the children, "join me?" Clumsily he fumbled back from the door and almost bumped into the stove.

"George, I've come to do some investigating. The day of the fire," the ranger's voice was abrupt, "did anybody come through the area—or how about the day before?"

"Er—er I'm not sure," the guard said.

"The day of the arsonist fire," the ranger's voice dropped soberly, "the fire control chief doesn't have any record of your spotting the fire at all. The guard on Dirtyface Mountain lookout saw the fire before you did. But your lookout station is closer to the fire area—didn't you even see any smoke?"

Lookout George Olson pushed his glasses higher on his bony nose. His arms were frail and his forest service uniform drooped from his thin frame. "Well, Ranger Lewis," he hesitated nervously holding the door knob, "that day I was preparing information packets in case any tourists came through. And I—I guess I just forgot to patrol the forest that day. But I really will try harder, sir," the guard's voice faltered. "I really am grateful you let me have this job."

The ranger's voice was stern, but not unkind. "First you almost fell a tree on yourself and now this. You've got to try harder, George. The whole Chiwawa forest could have gone up in flames while you were preparing information packets for tourists.

"Speaking of tourists—did any come through that day or the day before?"

George Olson pushed thin strands of straight, sparse hair back from his high forehead, "I—I don't think so, sir. I don't ever see many tourists. Old George's sign usually scares them away."

"So besides Old George and you there was nobody in the area as far as you know," the ranger persisted.

When her uncle mentioned Old George, Ann noticed a strange, inscrutable expression flicker in George Olson's eyes. He peered apprehensively at the ranger through his thick smudged glasses. "I never see Old George, Ranger Lewis," the guard said. "He—he won't speak to me."

When they were finally back inside the pickup, past Old George's gate, and on the road to Lake Wenatchee again, Uncle Jack sighed deeply. "Talk about two strange characters! And both of them named George. First Old George the miner and then this character, George Olson."

The ranger turned that day's investigation over in his mind. "I can't figure that George Olson out," he said aloud. "I've never seen anybody want a job so badly. For two years he's been begging me for a guard job and he insisted on Red Mountain Mine.

"Olson was vague about his past jobs. He's had a lot of education but no experience in the woods. But he was so persistent, I hired him to work at Red Mountain Mine. He's a likable fellow, but if he'd only pay more attention to what he's doing! One month in the forest and he's almost managed to kill himself and burn the forest!"

"I think I'll go for a walk," Robb announced that night after supper.

"Robb—where are you going? Can I come with you?" Ann followed her brother.

"Oh, nowhere important," he shrugged. "Just thought I'd cool off. I think I'll just go by myself if you don't mind."

Ann followed her brother to the door, out of earshot of Aunt Betty and Uncle Jack who were sitting on the terrace overlooking the lake. "I do mind," she hissed. "I know where you're going. You want to meet some of the boys from the bunkhouse up on the hill. I want to come too."

"Well, Freckles," Robb tried to annoy his sister into staying home, "hurry up—if you have to come." When he saw Ann reach for her jacket, he pushed roughly out the door. "I'll never meet anybody with you along."

The children walked silently through the darkness up the hill toward the thick trees bordering the bunkhouse. Through the trees in the distance, Ann heard voices. "Some of the boys are out walking, too . . . it will be easier for us to get acquainted," she thought gladly.

But then Robb slowed to a stop. Impatiently she motioned him forward—why did he always have to hesitate? Robb's fingers flew to his lips, "Quiet!" He leaned forward noiselessly against the pine trees.

Through the branches, Ann spied two young crewmen sitting on the ground, their backs propped on the trees, talking in the dark. "If you ask me, I think that grumpy old miner is the guilty one," one of the boys speculated loudly. "I wouldn't be surprised if he set that fire out of orneriness. Old George swears he's going to get even with the ranger for letting tourists in."

The other boy lit a cigarette and motioned toward the trees. Ann slunk from the shadows. "If you ask me I think it was that Red Mountain guard George Olson who set the fire," the boy muttered. "He's really odd."

The boy blew cigarette smoke into the night and spoke slowly. "A few days ago the ranger told me to deliver supplies to George Olson at Red Mountain Mine lookout station. Olson wasn't inside the lookout so I started searching for him. Guess where I found him? Snooping around Old George's cabin . . . peeking inside the window! He looked mighty suspicious!"

"Maybe Old George and George Olson are in cahoots," the first voice said. The boy with the cigarette stood. Tensely Ann tiptoed after Robb away from the trees.

The children hurried silently back toward the ranger house. "Wow!" Robb stopped when they were safely beyond the boys' bunkhouse. "What do you think of that? We didn't make any new friends, but we sure heard a lot. They suspect George Olson."

"And they suspect Old George," Ann reminded her brother. "I wonder if they saw him sneaking around the fire too."

Inside the ranger station house, Aunt Betty rolled crust for a blackberry pie. Uncle Jack was settled in his office downstairs, filling out a timber report.

"Let's go outside," Robb jerked his head in the direction of the terrace. "We better decide what we should tell Uncle Jack and Aunt Betty—if we should tell them at all."

For a long time Robb and Ann sat on the terrace talking about the arsonist and that day's evidence. Lights from the summer cabins and campfires along Lake Wenatchee's shores twinkled on the sleeping lake.

One of the lights on the opposite shore burned more brightly than the others. As Ann watched, the ball of brightness seemed to slowly explode in the black night. "Robb," Ann said, "that light. It's so big!"

"Probably just a campfire," he yawned, but Robb sauntered to the railing and studied the yellow spot in the distance. He stiffened. "That's fire—and it's burning fast!" he shouted. "Quick, we'd better warn Uncle Jack!"

6 Brian's Discovery

"Uncle Jack!" Robb's face burned with excitement, "Quick! I think we've spotted a forest fire on the south shore!"

"It's probably just a campfire that the children see, Jack," Aunt Betty dusted pie crust flour from her hands.

The ranger grabbed his binoculars from the shelf by the forest service radio. Out on the terrace, he focused the binoculars on the fire. In a few strides he was back at the radio calling the fire control chief.

"4-11! 4-11! Emergency fire call!" he spoke tersely into the radio receiver. "It's over on south shore. Rouse five men from the bunkhouse. Load the equipment into the pickups. We'll leave immediately!"

Uncle Jack turned to Robb who stood tensely at his side. "Robb—you better stay home. You know tomorrow is Sunday and you said you wanted to go to church in the morning. It depends on how big that fire is —but we could end up fighting it all night!"

"Jack, the boy will be exhausted by morning," Aunt Betty worried.

"I don't want to miss church, Uncle Jack," Robb's eyes searched his uncle's face, "but I'm not tired. Even if we stay out late I can still go to church tomorrow. I want to help. Besides, I couldn't sleep anyway!"

"Quick then!" Uncle Jack grabbed his orange hard hat with the forest service seal from a hook on the wall, and shoved another tin hat toward Robb.

Ann wandered back to the terrace. She leaned into the cool caressing breeze blowing from the lake. The spot on the south shore flamed orange and menacing. "O, God, please help them reach the fire before it destroys more of the forest . . . before it hurts the animals. Please keep Uncle Jack and Robb safe . . ." she leaned her head against the railing as she prayed.

The next morning Ann helped her aunt set the table and waited eagerly for her uncle and Robb to waken. "Do you know what time they came home, Aunt Betty?" Ann asked.

"A little after midnight," Uncle Jack interrupted as he appeared suddenly in the kitchen door. "Thanks to you and Robb," he smiled at Ann, "we reached that fire before it raged out of control."

"You knew I spotted the fire too?" Ann asked shyly.

"Robb told me you spotted it first out on the terrace," the ranger laid his arm proudly on his nephew's shoulder. "I don't know what we would have done last night without Robb. He's turning into quite a fire fighter."

Aunt Betty looked as if she disapproved of boys Robb's age fighting fire, but she managed a brief smile. "We knew we were gaining a niece and nephew for the summer, but I never imagined you two city children would turn out to be forest service lookouts," Aunt Betty complimented them.

"Uncle Jack," Ann hesitated, "do you know yet how last night's fire started? Was it set on purpose by the arsonist—like the one up Chiwawa River Road?"

"No," Uncle Jack replied thoughtfully, "we can't blame this one on the arsonist. It looks to me like some careless campers caused this one. The campers evidently left the campsite before they made sure their fire was completely extinguished."

"Do people or lightning cause more fires?" Ann wondered.

"People," Uncle Jack replied gravely. "Nine out of ten forest fires are caused by man, not nature. Last year 100,000 fires burned and scarred about 3,000,000 acres. About 90% of those fires are the fault of human beings. Every year enough trees are destroyed to supply the building needs of a city of 250,000 people."

"And so much beauty is destroyed," Aunt Betty spoke more gently than usual.

When Ann asked her aunt an hour later if she would like to come to church that Sunday, Aunt Betty answered tersely, "No, maybe another Sunday; I've got to freeze the peas from the garden today."

"I'll drive them down to the church," Uncle Jack volunteered, and momentarily Ann hoped her uncle would come with them to church. But before Ann could ask, her uncle added, "I'll drop you at the church, and then I must check the fire."

As they drove along the lake through the mountains, Ann watched eagerly for the church—the only one in the little community of Lake Wenatchee, Aunt Betty had said. They turned a sloping corner, and crossed a graceful bridge suspended above a shimmering river. Loose planks on the wooden bridge tinkled like a marimba as they drove across. On the other side of the river a trim white church peeked through the pine trees.

"We don't know anyone," Robb whispered reluctantly when Uncle Jack had driven from the church yard. But the church looked so friendly that Ann did not feel timid. A sign said, "Lake Wenatchee Community Church."

"I'm going to call this church 'the Chapel in the Pines,' " Ann told her brother.

Hearty singing echoed joyfully into the woods from an open window at the front of the church. Gently Ann pushed the pine wood door and stepped into the chapel. "O Lord my God . . . How great Thou art . . ." The majestic words of the hymn soared out the open window to the sparkling blue sky.

The young pastor opened his black Bible and placed it in the pinewood pulpit before him. "God created the world—a perfect world. God created a pure and holy man to live in this world," the pastor said. "But man purposely disobeyed God and filled the world with destruction and heartache.

"God loved man so much, He sent His own Son, Jesus Christ, to die for our sins. Now no matter how bad we have been, Christ loves us and wants to make us new creatures before we destroy ourselves, others—and even the world we live in."

After the service a tall muscular man in a Sunday suit and logger's boots gripped Robb's hand. "So you're Ranger Lewis' nephew—and here's his niece. I'm Mr. Madson." The strong, friendly logger motioned to a tousle-haired, tanned boy beside him, "And this is my son, Brian." Ann noticed Brian's face, sprinkled with freckles—not as many as she had, but somehow Brian's freckles only made his face seem friendly.

Robb recognized the boy only a little older than himself. His voice filled with admiration, "You're the one who saved George Olson's life when the tree almost fell on him at the Chiwawa fire!" Robb exclaimed.

Soon the three children were huddled together like old friends in the church courtyard discussing the mysterious fire. "Who do you think it was?" Ann whispered. Robb leaned against the sturdy pine tree which held the big church bell in its wide branches. A striped chipmunk, annoyed at all the people who had invaded its forest, squeaked protests from a branch on the bell tree.

Brian answered Ann's question with a puzzled frown. "Most of the people I know think it's Old George. My dad and most of the people here at church think he's guilty. But . . ." Brian hesitated as if he were deciding whether to confide completely in Ann and Robb, "I'm not sure."

Brian's voice dropped to a whisper as he leaned further into the trees. "A strange thing happened," he said. "My dad is logging in the woods not far from Old George's cabin. One night after the logging crew went home, I stayed on alone at the cut to fire watch for my dad."

"Fire watch?" Ann was puzzled.

"During the extreme fire danger season," Brian explained, "the law says that someone from the logging crew must stay and patrol the logging area for several hours after we shut down for the day in case a fire starts.

"That night while I was patrolling the logging area," Brian continued his story, "I detoured near Old George's cabin. Through the moonlight, I saw two shadowy figures standing by the cabin. I think one of the men was Old George. The other man, whose face I didn't see, handed something to Old George. Through the moonlight, the object looked like—a kerosene can."

"A kerosene can!" Ann gasped. "But that's how the arsonist started the fire."

"I know," Brian said softly.

7 An Evasive
Archaeologist

After that first Sunday, Robb and Ann saw Brian every Sunday at the Chapel in the Pines. One Monday Brian's father dropped him off at the ranger house on their way home from work in the woods.

"We've been waiting for you," Robb met Brian at the door. "Hurry and change. Let's go for a swim!" Brian, dusty from his day clearing brush in the woods, plunged first into the clear, chilly lake.

After supper, the three children sprawled out on the terrace eating blackberry tarts and trying to solve the mystery of the fire.

"My dad still thinks it's Old George. I've

heard some people say the old miner probably set the fire just out of spite—to keep people away. But I don't think so," Brian mused. "I think Old George loves the forest too much to do that."

As the sun edged slowly down the sky, Brian talked about his life in the mountains. "My parents have always lived here," he explained, "and my grandparents before them. My great grandparents came to Lake Wenatchee from Pennsylvania.

"When they saw our valley—well, I guess they just figured the valley was too beautiful to travel any farther. My great grandfather was one of the first settlers in Lake Wenatchee valley—they called it homesteading."

"Wow," Ann's imagination carried her back to the pioneers who had settled the valley, "it would have been fun to live then!"

"Well, I think you're lucky to live at Lake Wenatchee now," Robb envied Brian. "I wish I lived here instead of Chicago."

"I think I could live at Lake Wenatchee forever," Ann stretched her arms.

"What about your freckles?" Robb grinned. "You said yourself they bloom like flowers under the mountain sun. You might just turn into one big freckle!"

"You are horrid!" Ann blushed at her brother's remarks in front of Brian. But then she remembered Brian's face brown with freckles and felt a little consoled.

"I—I don't think freckles are so bad, Robb," Brian said kindly when he saw Ann's confusion. "My mother says they make my face more interesting than plain faces," he glanced shyly at Ann.

"Are you going to stay here in the valley —forever, Brian?" Ann asked timidly.

Brian pulled closer a pine bough that hung over the terrace. He picked three green pine needles and thoughtfully braided them together.

"I used to think I would live here forever," he reflected, "but then three years ago things changed for me. At vacation Bible school that summer I became a Christian. I'd always gone to the Chapel in the Pines as you call it, Ann, and my parents are Christians. But before then I didn't really know God. I hadn't ever asked Christ to forgive my sins and be my guide.

"Now as much as I love the valley," Brian said soberly, "I am not sure I can stay here all my life. I think God wants me to go to school—to be a preacher and tell others about Him. That probably means I would have to move away from the valley."

"Maybe God will bring you back to be the preacher at the Chapel in the Pines," Ann said wistfully.

Uncle Jack's heavy footsteps thudded on the terrace. "I can tell from your purple tongues you've eaten all Aunt Betty's blackberry tarts," he teased.

Uncle Jack leaned against the terrace railing. "How would you three like to go up to Dirtyface lookout station tomorrow?" he said abruptly. "The lookout, Bruce Morgan, has run out of supplies and Cleo, the packer, plans to carry them up tomorrow."

"I wish I could go, Mr. Lewis," Brian thanked the ranger, "but Dad's short on logging help this summer. Thanks anyway."

Ann turned to look at the formidable dark mountain named Dirtyface which loomed behind the ranger station. She had wanted to climb it ever since the first morning when she had wakened and seen the sun playing at its peak. "Uncle Jack," she gulped, "I want to go, but how big are the packs we have to carry up to the lookout station?"

Brian and Uncle Jack laughed merrily. Even Robb was laughing. "The horses carry the packs," Robb explained importantly. "You really are a city girl," Robb joked.

Ann blushed, "Don't forget you're from the city too," she poked her brother.

"The horses will carry you and the packs," Uncle Jack explained, "but they can't do all the work. You'd better get some sleep; 5:30 will come early. Cleo wants to leave the ranger station while the morning is still cool."

The next morning, Ann recognized Cleo, the packer, from the time she had seen him loading the pack horses on Chiwawa River Road. He wore high boots and a broad crumpled cowboy hat which curled up on one side and down the other over his bushy gray hair. Ann thought the packer looked far too old to still be climbing mountains, but he lifted the heavy packs easily onto the horses' backs.

When the packs of food and other supplies for the lookout guard were all tied securely on the backs of the patient horses, Cleo looped a lead rope between them. "Keeps 'em together that way," Cleo explained. Effortlessly the packer stepped into the stirrup and settled in the saddle.

Ann watched with admiration as Robb slid into his saddle as swiftly as if he had been riding horses all his life. Cautiously Ann stepped into the stirrup while her uncle held the horse's bridle.

"Old Star won't run away with you," Uncle Jack encouraged. "She's been at the ranger station almost as long as Cleo. Cleo's so fond of Old Star that he named his granddaughter 'Star Rose' after his horse."

"Pretty name, isn't it?" Cleo smiled proudly.

Ann was glad they had started early. Already the sun glistened warmly through the pines. The trail sloped gradually upward at first, but then turned suddenly steep. Star plodded along slowly and Ann clung to the saddle. "Don't worry—it won't slide," Cleo reassured. "That saddle's cinched tight around the horse's belly."

"Were you here—even before Uncle Jack came to Lake Wenatchee ranger station?" Robb asked the packer.

"I was here before your uncle even thought about being a ranger," Cleo chuckled. "When I went to work on the Lake Wenatchee district there weren't any roads —just trails. In my day there was just one ranger for the whole forest. He built the trails, fought the fires, and looked after everything himself.

"The first ranger even named many of the places around here. He named three of the lakes in this district—Mary, Lois, and Jane—for his sisters. See those two peaks over there?" Cleo pulled his horse to a halt on the trail and pointed with a bent finger toward the west. "Those two peaks were so close together the ranger named them David and Jonathan after the friends in the Bible story."

"How did Dirtyface get its name?" Ann asked as her horse plodded up the hill.

"Well, the way I heard the story," Cleo said, "the men who used to haul timber off the mountain in the pioneering days came down from the mountain every evening with dust and dirt streaked on their faces. I guess it was their wives who named the mountain 'Dirtyface.' "

Ann saw the tiny lookout station through the trees long before they reached the frame building on top of the peak.

The lookout guard, Bruce Morgan, hurried out of his house as if he were glad for company. "Come on in and have a look around," Bruce invited with a smile when they had unloaded the packs. While the packer led the horses down the slope to graze and find water, Ann and Robb followed the lookout guard inside.

The small cabin was simple—one room walled by windows. A compass instrument stood in the center of the room. "What's this?" Robb bent to study the dial.

"That's the alidade—an instrument for determining the direction of a fire," Bruce explained. "Every three hours I survey the forest with high-power binoculars for any sign of fire. If I do spot anything—like that fire we had up the Chiwawa a few weeks ago—I use a map and the alidade to locate it exactly. Then I phone the location in to the ranger station at Lake Wenatchee."

Ann pressed close to the wide window. Before her the forest faded away endlessly. Below the forest she sighted the lake that lay like a puddle in the distance. The road along the lake twisted like a thin ribbon.

"Don't you get lonesome here?" Ann asked Bruce Morgan. "You don't have anybody to talk to." Ann was concerned.

"For my sister that would be the worst thing of all," Robb ignored Ann's frown.

Bruce laughed, "Sometimes I do miss having somebody to talk to. But here I have plenty of time to talk to God," Bruce said thoughtfully.

"You—you are a Christian!" Robb exclaimed joyfully. Soon Ann and Robb were telling Bruce how they had come from Chicago to spend the summer at Lake Wenatchee. Robb told Bruce about his uncle and aunt who were not Christians. Ann told him how they had discovered the little Chapel in the Pines and met Brian Madson.

At two o'clock Bruce glanced at his watch

and reached for his binoculars. "It's time for my forest check," he explained. The lookout guard surveyed the forest methodically through the binoculars. Suddenly he halted them in one direction. "Quick," he pulled Robb to the window. "Stand right there. Lift the binoculars. What do you see?"

"It's a man," Robb fumbled to adjust the binoculars. "I can't tell for sure but it looks like he has a shovel—like he's digging."

Bruce leaned his lanky shoulders against the wall by the two-way radio. "Something strange is going on," he murmured worriedly. "Day after day I see that fellow digging in the forest right near the area where the arsonist set the fire a few weeks ago.

"One day I hiked down to where the man was digging to get acquainted. He wasn't friendly. He finally told me he was an archaeologist and that he was digging for Indian artifacts. I'm interested in Indian history myself. I asked him if he had found any arrowheads. The archaeologist snapped, 'it's none of your business!' He told me to leave him alone and never bother him again.

"Every time I see that archaeologist, he's roaming around the area where the fire was set a few weeks ago. It's just a hunch," Bruce Morgan concluded, "but I'm suspicious of that fellow!"

8 A Fateful Camping Trip

All the way down the trail from Dirtyface Mountain, Ann pondered Bruce's words. So far all the evidence had seemed to point to Old George. She herself had seen the old miner at the site of the fire. Brian had seen somebody give Old George a kerosene can.

But what about this archaeologist—this secretive fellow who didn't want anybody to know why he was prowling around the forest? Ann recalled that Old George himself had suspected the archaeologist.

The weary horses zigzagged slowly down the steep mountain trail. Instinctively the animals knew the danger of descending too sharply down the slippery shale.

The hot sun faded slowly into the horizon, and by the time Ann, Robb, and Packer Cleo reached the ranger station the sky was only a gentle pink where the sun had hung.

The next morning when Ann awoke, she smelled blackberry pancakes from Aunt Betty's kitchen. She swung quickly from her bed, but her legs felt heavy. Stiffly she walked to the kitchen.

Uncle Jack smiled at her unsteady walk. "Now you can see why Cleo has bowlegs. He's spent half his life on horseback!"

That morning Mrs. Madson called Aunt Betty. "Brian and his father and I are hiking up to Crescent Lake today and camping overnight," she explained. "We wondered if Robb and Ann would like to come along?"

Instantly Ann forgot her stiffness. "Please, Aunt Betty—can we go?" she begged.

"A sleeping bag for each of you. You can carry the sleeping bags and your other supplies in backpacks," Aunt Betty bustled around the living room—camping equipment strewn on the rug before her. "Be sure you have your quilted jackets. It's hot during the day, but the mountains turn cool at night."

"Jack," Aunt Betty turned anxiously to

her husband, "can you bring a compass for the children from the ranger station? The mountains aren't like Chicago. What would you city children ever do if you got lost?" Aunt Betty fretted.

The ranger saw the hurt in the children's eyes. "They're country children now, Betty," he reassured his anxious wife. "They've already hiked mountains and even fought fires. They'll manage!"

Before noon Brian Madson and his parents rumbled into the yard in their logger's pickup. "Ready?" Brian hollered from the open back of the pickup. After a last minute inventory by Aunt Betty to be certain their backpacks were complete, Ann and Robb clambered into the pickup beside Brian.

"Don't forget the compass. I put it in your backpack, Robb," Aunt Betty called after them as Brian's father steered the pickup out of the driveway.

As the pickup churned up Chiwawa River Road toward Crescent Lake campground, the children waved dust clouds away from their faces.

Then, when Brian's father had parked the pickup and the five of them started to climb the mountain, Ann felt her legs stiffen heavily. She had hated the ugly hiking boots Aunt Betty insisted on buying for her.

Now she felt the boots' sturdy support and was thankful.

The hikers talked little as they walked, and soon Ann found herself absorbed in the wonder world of the forest. Tall stately pines arched like pillars along the path. The slanting sunlight warmed the needles until they smelled spicy.

At last—when Ann thought she could hike no further—they reached Crescent Lake forest service campground. "Over this knoll," Mrs. Madson motioned the children a few yards farther to a small lake shaped like a crescent, cupped solitary and serene against the mountains.

Mr. Madson pulled a shovel, an ax, and a small plastic water bucket from his canvas pack. He found a flat spot and carefully scooped away the pine needles, grass, and roots. "Dad's clearing the ground cover," Brian explained, "so the campfire won't spread and become a forest fire. If the fire does start to burn out of control, we always carry a bucket along to douse the flames."

After supper each person washed his own tin plate, fork and spoon in lake water that Brian's mother had boiled. Mrs. Madson washed the stew can. "We never throw these away in the forest," she swished water around the can. "We use the cans for a kettle while we're camping, and then carry them back out in our packs to throw away."

Mr. Madson arranged the sleeping bags around the campfire. When the last embers glowed in the dying fire, he pulled his New Testament from his backpack and read from Psalms. "I will lift up mine eyes unto the hills, from whence cometh my help. My help cometh from the Lord, which made heaven and earth . . ."

When he had finished reading from the Bible, Mr. Madson prayed, "Thank You, God, for taking our lives which were sinful and ugly. Thank You for making them beautiful because of Your forgiveness . . ."

The next morning the campers slept until the sun beamed hot and insistent on their sleeping bags. After a steaming breakfast of pancakes and bacon, Brian had an idea for an exploration. "Years ago a railroad used to run from Red Mountain when the mine was operating. I bet there are lots of leaf fossils in the rock cut where the old railroad trestle used to be," he said eagerly.

"Don't forget the lunches I packed for you," Mrs. Madson reminded when the three children set out to find the old railroad.

"And don't get lost!" Mr. Madson added jokingly. "That old railroad trestle might not be so easy to find."

"Dad!" Brian was indignant. "You know I won't get lost! I've been raised in these woods all my life. I'll take care of Ann and Robb," he added protectively.

When the children had rambled about a mile beyond the lake, Ann discovered a patch of miniature berries among the pine needles. "They're wild strawberries," Brian explained.

"They're like fairy food," Ann exclaimed as she stooped to search for the tiny berries.

By noon the children still had not located the rock cut where the old railroad used to run. They sprawled on the grassy ground under a grove of lacy fir trees and hungrily ate their lunch. Ann wrapped two cookies inside her pocket, "in case I get hungry before we get back to camp," she thought.

Only when Ann felt the sun begin to cool did she look at her watch. "Brian! It's four o'clock. Your parents will be wondering what's happened to us!" she exclaimed anxiously.

"Ann, you're as bad as Aunt Betty," Robb grumbled. "You're always worrying. We're not little kids! Besides if you're so worried," Robb grinned at his sister, "you should have made a trail of freckles we could follow back to camp. You have enough to spare!"

In speechless rage, Ann stomped down the hill after Brian. "I'm glad at least *Brian* knows the way back to the camp," she muttered in her fury.

Slowly the sun dropped behind the mountain. Brian walked steadily, but not with the same certainty as he had before. He hesitated in the darkening forest. His voice tightened strangely, "Robb—Ann, do you remember this grove of fir trees? Is this where we ate lunch? It's getting dark so fast I can't find the path." Brian's voice quavered, "I—I'm afraid we're lost!"

9 Dangerous Shelter

"Lost!" Ann felt like screaming for help into the dark night. Terror clutched her. Through the darkness, Ann saw fear flicker across Robb's face.

Brian's voice faltered, "It was stupid of me not to watch the time. I was trying so hard to find that rock cut with the fossils, I forgot to watch the sun. I knew we'd come a long way from camp, but I figured we wouldn't have any trouble finding the way back."

"But our compass," Ann turned happily to her brother. Futilely, Robb reached into his pocket, "I have my New Testament, but I guess I left the compass in the pack back at camp," he admitted.

"Oh, Robb . . ." Ann wailed, "and after Aunt Betty told us we should always carry the compass with us. She will really think we are city kids now!"

By this time Brian had recovered his usual confidence and he spoke with authority. "It's getting dark and we might as well admit we're lost. If we try to find our way out now, we will end up more lost. We have to find a shelter where we can spend the night."

"But wild animals . . . we'll freeze to death . . ." fears surged in Ann's mind.

Instead of telling his sister not to be a coward, as he usually might have, Robb's voice was kind and protective. "Let—let's pray before we look for a shelter."

The three children knelt beside a cold, flat rock. "Dear God," Robb prayed, "please help us to find a shelter tonight and a way out of the forest tomorrow. Please help us find Brian's parents again. Help them to not be afraid. . . ."

Back by Crescent Lake, Mrs. Madson paced around the campfire. Her husband sat hunched by the campfire, quietly praying.

"If they were not lost they would have

found their way back by now," Mrs. Madson said tearfully.

"It's a good thing Brian has grown up in the forest," Mr. Madson tried to comfort his wife, but his own voice trembled. "If they're not back shortly after the sun comes out tomorrow morning, I'm hiking out to ask a search party to come help us look around for them."

Mr. Madson reached for his wife's hand, "Let's pray now and ask God to protect them and bring them home by morning."

Mrs. Madson lay in her warm sleeping bag, but she shivered. Her eyes on the heavens, she prayed for the three children lost in the night.

"It's so dark we can't move far to look for a shelter," Brian decided. "Ann, you stand right here," he commanded. "Robb, you walk along this side of the cliff, and I'll explore the other direction for a shelter."

Robb groped along the shadowy outlines of the shale cliff. Quickly he swerved away from the solid stone toward a bush hedged against the cliff.

"Help! Help!" Robb screamed as the prickly bush collapsed and he felt his body tumbling into the cliff.

"It's a cave!" Brian yelled when he discovered Robb picking himself up from the hole beyond the bent bush. "You've fallen into a big cave. It must be an old mine shaft. We've found our shelter for the night," Brian exclaimed happily.

"Do you really think it's safe to stay here all night?" Ann hesitated at the hole opening into the cliffs. "What if this is somebody's hideaway?"

Robb had forgotten his bruises from the fall. "Don't be silly, Ann," he said importantly since he was the one who had actually discovered the cave, "this is a perfect shelter!"

"I'm glad your mother made us take our quilted jackets along," Robb admitted to Brian. He pulled the warm coat close around his shoulders as the children huddled inside the cave.

Ann pulled her two cookies from her pocket, "And I'm glad I didn't eat these at lunch," she said.

"We can't eat them now," Brian answered the unspoken question of the three hungry children.

"We'll divide one for breakfast. We will have to save the other one in case it takes us all day to get out . . ." his voice trailed off into the dark forest.

That night Ann stretched out just inside the entrance of the cave. Through the cave door, she fixed her eyes on the stars. "At least they haven't moved," she thought. Ann prayed as she studied the stars. She thought she was far too frightened and cold to sleep, but slowly exhaustion from the fearful day sapped her strength—and to her own surprise she slept.

The three children slept until the warm, welcome sun shone like a searchlight into the cave door. "We'll find our way out fast now that the sun's up—won't we?" Ann asked hopefully.

Ann shook her body, stiff from lying on the cold dirt floor of the cave. She combed her tangled hair with her fingers. She braided it into one long braid that fell down her back and tied the braid with her handkerchief.

Brian rose to leave the cave, but Robb had a sudden suggestion. "Before we go let's just take a look and see how far back this cave goes. Maybe we can tell if it was an old mining shaft."

Robb slipped back into the high dark cave—now partially lit by the sunlight. Reluctantly Ann followed Brian as he walked back into the cave.

"Brian! Ann!" Ahead in the cave, Ann heard Robb's insistent voice and a thudding metal sound.

"Quick, look what's stacked here," Robb's voice echoed back. He thumped the cans again.

Along the side of the cave several kerosene cans stood in neat rows. "BOGGS" the label across the front read when they held the can up to the sunlight.

"Those are the same kind of cans the arsonist left behind when he set the fire up Chiwawa River Road!" Robb's voice began to rise excitedly.

"But why are all of them stacked here?" Ann asked, puzzled.

Brian's face grew grave. "I—I'm afraid we may have stumbled on the arsonist's hideout. Maybe he has all these new cans of kerosene stashed away here to start more fires. The old ones are probably from the other fire. It looks like he's hidden the evidence here."

"Let's get away from here—I'm scared," Ann felt terror tighten her body.

But in the same moment, all three of the children heard a crackling sound in the distance. "It's the bush at the entrance," Robb whispered, his voice frantic. "Somebody's coming in the cave!"

"Quick!" Brian's voice was urgent. "Follow me. Don't make a sound. We can't escape from the cave now."

Silently the children creeped back to where the cave turned a corner.

Slow, heavy footsteps thudded closer . . . and closer.

10 A Special Reunion

Mrs. Madson took her Bible and settled herself against a sturdy fir tree beside Crescent Lake. She glanced apprehensively at the sun, which she had watched grow brighter since the first crack of light at five o'clock that morning, when her husband had set off down the trail to tell Ranger Jack that the children were lost.

"I'll hike down to Red Mountain lookout station where George Olson is guard and call the ranger on the forest service radio. That's the closest phone. I'll ask Ranger Jack to organize a search team of four other men and hike back in with me immediately.

Maybe by the time we get back," Mr. Madson had managed a smile, "the children will be here, too."

Later that morning Mrs. Madson heard hasty footsteps approaching the camp. She ran toward the trail, but she knew from the loud pounding sounds that the search party —not the children—had arrived back at camp.

Three foresters followed behind Mr. Madson. One carried a portable forest service radio. Then Mrs. Madson saw Ranger Lewis and his wife Betty coming up the trail.

"Betty!" Mrs. Madson threw her arms warmly around the children's aunt. "I'm glad you've come with the men!"

Betty Lewis, who was not a woman accustomed to crying, brushed away tears. "I'm just so worried about the children. I thought I might as well come along and help look instead of sitting moping at home. I am so frightened—and there's nowhere to turn for help!" her voice trailed off in anguish into the silent forest.

"There is one place," Mr. Madson said softly. He slipped his arm around his wife's shoulder. "Ever since we knew last night that the children were lost, we've been praying to God for help. We believe He will help us."

"And I'm sure the children are praying too," Mrs. Madson added softly.

"Before we set out to search," Mr. Madson turned to the ranger and the three foresters, "let's pray and ask God to guide us to the children."

The three foresters glanced at the ranger and then bowed their heads uncertainly. The ranger hesitated a moment. Then he dropped to his knees in the soft mountain grass and bowed his head while Brian's father prayed.

The children clung to the wall of the cave. Ann wished the dirt walls would open and hide them from the arsonist. "Do you think he knows we're here?" Ann whispered, but Brian's finger flew in a warning to his lips.

Ann shuddered at every threatening footstep. "Please, Lord," she prayed silently, "help the arsonist stop before he comes around this corner. . . ."

Suddenly Ann heard the clatter of metal. The arsonist had stopped—at the stockpile of kerosene cans. For several seconds the children heard clanging sounds as the arsonist fumbled with the cans.

"I'll have to carry the rest out later," the arsonist grunted to himself loudly enough that the children overheard. With relief, the children heard the arsonist's footsteps recede back out the entrance of the cave.

Ann wanted to run for the cave door into the safe sunshine as soon as the footsteps had died away. She turned toward the opening, but Robb jerked her back with a motion of his hand. "Quiet," he hissed. "We can't go out yet. We have to be sure he's really gone. What if he's waiting at the cave door? He'll grab us!"

Ann slumped back against the cave wall. She knew Robb was right. There was nothing to do but wait—wait until it was safe to leave the cave. "But how long do we have to wait?" she whispered anxiously.

"Sh-sh . . ." was Robb's only reply.

After many minutes, Brian whispered, "I'll lead the way. I'll try to look from an angle when we get near the door to be sure the arsonist isn't waiting outside."

Trembling, Ann followed the boys. She stepped quietly in case the man still lurked somewhere near. Brian peered carefully out one side of the cave. Then he silently surveyed the other side. Like a scout, he motioned Ann and Robb out of the cave with his hand.

Ann held her breath and dashed through the cave door—heedlessly shoving the bush aside. She wanted to run and run and not stop until the frightening cave was far behind her.

"Wow!" Brian said when he had slowly caught his breath and the children were safely beyond the cave. "That was scary! Am I ever glad that the arsonist—whoever he is—didn't come any further. A few more steps and he would have discovered that we had stumbled onto his hideout!"

"I prayed and asked God to protect us. Thank you, God," Ann said simply.

Robb's voice was urgent, "Did you hear that arsonist say he was coming back 'to get the rest later'? We've got to get out of these woods fast and tell Uncle Jack. I think Uncle Jack would like to meet the arsonist."

"I wouldn't," Ann shuddered. "I hope we don't run into him in the forest."

Brian studied the sun. "See how this ravine slopes west? If we follow the sun down the ravine we should come out on the Chiwawa River Road. From there we can find our way back to camp."

"But we better make some markers— maybe with pinecones—so we can find our way back to the arsonist's hideout," Robb reminded.

Fright of the arsonist had so enveloped Ann that she had forgotten how hungry she was. All she had eaten for several hours was a third of the chocolate chip cookie the children had divided that morning. As the hot sun burned into her tired body, she longed for water and food. "Are we almost near Chiwawa Road?" Wearily she followed Brian's zigzag trail down the ridge.

Before Brian could answer, all three children heard the sinister crackle of footsteps approaching. Brian sunk into the trees, "It might be the arsonist again! Hide quick!"

But the trees did not conceal the children. In a few moments an old hunched man with a shotgun slung across his shoulder stood before them.

"Old George!" Ann gasped.

"So it's the ranger's kids," the old man wheezed. "What are yuh doin' skulking around my woods—don't yuh know this here's private property?" the old man remarked irritably, but he lowered his shotgun.

"We—we are lost, sir," Brian's voice floundered.

"Hmpf . . ." the old man squinted at Brian. "Ain't you Logger Madson's kid? Grew up in the forest all yer life. Lost! That's a likely story!"

"But we are lost," desperate tears brimmed in Ann's eyes. "We're lost and hungry and thirsty—and besides," tears splattered down her face, "we've been lost the whole night and we had to sleep in a ca—" Ann started to say, but then with a piercing look from Robb she quickly remembered that Old George might be the arsonist. She shouldn't tell him they had slept in the arsonist's hideout.

"We slept all night in the forest," she recovered her sentence, "and we don't want to trespass on your property—all we want to do is get back to our camp." Tears flooded down her cheeks.

"Well, now, don't cry, little girl," Old George's voice was almost gentle. "Yuh might wash away all them pretty freckles."

"Do—do you really think freckles are pretty?" Ann's eyes widened through her tears.

"Yup, I guess I'd say I do . . ." Old George's voice trailed away strangely, but then he turned gruffly to the children. "So yuh ain't had nothing to eat," he said as if the children's hunger were their own fault. "Yuh might as well come on along to my cabin. Won't be like yer used to at home, but yuh won't go away hungry neither."

Ann was surprised to find her fear disappearing. Eagerly she followed the old miner into his wood cabin that slumped crookedly between some spruce trees. Inside, the cabin was musty and dark except for a few slants of window light which rested uncertainly on the lopsided wood table and two benches—the only furniture in the room beside a bed in one corner and a wood burning stove in the other.

Old George propped his shotgun against the wall and pulled some kindling from under the wood stove. In a few minutes, fire crackled in the stove. Ann leaned her head on the splintery table. When she awoke a pile of pancakes was heaped on a tin plate in front of her.

" 'Tain't much, but them sour doughs will fill yuh up 'til yer uncle gets here," the old man poured more pancake batter into the black iron frying pan.

Even Aunt Betty's blackberry pancakes had never tasted so good, Ann decided as she poured the thick syrup Old George had cooked over the pancakes.

"Well," Old George grumbled when the children had eaten plates of pancakes, "if yuh won't eat no more of my sour doughs, I guess I'll have to think of some way to get yuh home."

"Home! Oh, thank you, Mr. . . . er . . . Old George," Ann hesitated.

For the first time a smile crinkled at the corner of the old man's mouth. "That's all right. I can hardly remember muh last name myself anymore. Old George's good enough.

"Well," the old man shrugged when they stood outside his cabin, "I ain't got no car and it's a long walk out from here back to yer camp. I figure the best thing's if we build a fire out of green boughs. They'll make only a few flames but lots of smoke. I'll pour a little kerosene on to get her burnin'."

"Fire! Kerosene!" Robb exclaimed when the old man had disappeared inside his cabin to find a blanket. "Maybe Old George is the arsonist!"

"He is not," Ann said stubbornly.

"How do you know?" Robb taunted. "Just because he said he liked your freckles. . . ."

The miner emerged from the cabin with an old blanket. "Once we get the smoke billowin', I'll use the blanket to signal. That city slicker lookout guard down at Red Mountain Mine won't be able to miss that. When he sees smoke, he'll come scootin' up here fast enough to see what's wrong. Then he ken radio yer uncle.

"Yuh better start gathering boughs for the fire," Old George reminded the children gruffly, " 'less yuh want to end up stayin' here all night!"

"I—I think it would be nice if we could

come stay in your cabin sometime," Ann smiled at the old miner. An expression almost gentle swept across Old George's face.

Abruptly the old man turned his back and busied himself with the fire. Soon smoke spiraled up from the fire. Old George interrupted the smoke with the blanket so that it rose in three big puffs.

"They'll come all right when they see the smoke," Old George had predicted, and a half hour later Ann heard the rumble of a pickup. Happily she spotted the familiar forest service emblem on the side of the green pickup.

"I saw the smoke signal and came right away," George Olson said as soon as he stepped out of the pickup. He glanced for approval to Old George.

"I'm going to radio the ranger right now and tell him I've found you," George Olson scurried back to the pickup. He returned in a few minutes from his conversation on the two-way radio. "The search party is on their way down to Chiwawa River Road. The ranger is so glad I found you," the forester said proudly. "You were really lost."

"But we're found now," Ann exclaimed joyfully as she started to climb the high step into the pickup. Suddenly she stepped back down. "Robb—that New Testament you have in your jacket. Let's give it to Old George," she said impulsively.

The two children returned to thank the old man who had rescued and fed them. Shyly, Robb gave the old man the New Testament.

"I'll never believe Old George is the arsonist," Ann thought to herself when they were back inside the pickup, and George Olson was nervously winding the vehicle down Chiwawa Road.

Forester George Olson halted the pickup beside the trail leading up to Crescent Lake campground. "No," the forester's glasses slid uncertainly down his nose when Robb asked if they could hike up the trail to meet their uncle and Brian's parents. "Your uncle said we were supposed to stay right here and wait for him. He said he didn't want all four of us getting lost."

But shortly the search party came hurrying down the trail. "Thank the Lord you're found!" Mrs. Madson enclosed all three of the children in her arms at once.

"Yes, I'm thankful to—to God, too," Aunt Betty said as she hugged the children.

"But, Jack, those children can't hike back with you to the cave after all they've been through," Aunt Betty interrupted when Robb told the story of the arsonist's cave. "They're exhausted."

"Ann can go with you back to the ranger station," the ranger's voice was sober, "but, Betty, if the boys heard the arsonist say he's returning, we'll have to hike back to that cave as quickly as possible. If that really is the arsonist toting kerosene cans out of the cave, we've got to catch him fast before he starts any more fires!"

The ranger strode to his pickup and spoke into his two-way radio, "This is Ranger Lewis calling Lake Wenatchee ranger station. I have a message for you to relay to the sheriff. . . ."

Back at the ranger station Ann washed and slept and then settled on the terrace beside her aunt to wait for her uncle and Robb. She stared over the railing into the maple bushes by the lake. Although she had watched for her fawn every day, he hadn't come again.

"It can't be Old George," Ann mused about the mystery of the kerosene cans in the cave. "He was kind to us, and he looked almost happy when we gave him the New Testament. But who was that man in the hideout cave if it wasn't Old George?"

It was almost dark when the ranger's pickup finally turned into the ranger station yard. "It's not Old George, is it?" Ann ran apprehensively to her uncle and Robb.

"No, it's not Old George," her uncle's voice was haggard, "but the mystery—thanks to you two 'country kids' and Brian—is solved."

"Did the arsonist come back to the cave? Was it his hideout? Who was the arsonist?" Ann's questions tumbled over each other.

"Whoa . . ." Uncle Jack smiled and sat down at the kitchen table. "How about some coffee, Betty," he spoke to his wife, "and then I'll unravel the whole mystery for you and Ann.

"You remember the archaeologist—or so-called archaeologist—that Old George had seen sneaking around his property?" Uncle Jack asked.

"The same one that Bruce Morgan, the lookout on Dirtyface Mountain, suspected!" Ann exclaimed.

"Well," Uncle Jack continued, "they were both right. This fellow pretended he was an archaeologist so nobody would know why he was digging around the mountains, but he was really prospecting for gold. He did discover some gold—but the gold was on Old George's land.

"The fake archaeologist knew he could never dig out the gold as long as Old George lived on the land. To get rid of old George, the archaeologist decided to frame him—to set a fire and make it look like the old miner was guilty. He knew everybody would suspect Old George, and he thought if he could get him arrested and taken to prison then he would be free to dig out the gold on Old George's land."

"But why did Old George have one of the cans of kerosene at his house the first time you went to question him?" Ann puzzled.

"The archaeologist purposely left the two cans of BOGGS KEROSENE by the fire so that we would discover them. Then as a supposedly friendly gesture, he gave a can of kerosene to Old George."

"The archaeologist! That's who Brian must have seen in the moonlight handing the kerosene can to Old George," Ann interrupted her uncle.

"Well, the archaeologist is the one who gave Old George the BOGGS kerosene," the ranger continued. "He knew the old miner was poor and would probably accept his gift. And I suppose he hoped that whoever came to investigate would also see the kerosene can. He hoped this would incriminate Old George for sure. The arsonist never guessed that you three would stumble into his hideout and discover where his real supply was stored."

"And he never guessed he would be in

jail," Robb added. "When the sheriff arrested him, the archaeologist was still trying to blame Old George."

"If there's gold on Old George's land—does that mean he's rich now?" Ann wondered.

"In more ways than one," Uncle Jack chuckled. "I haven't told you the whole story yet. On the way back down from the cave, Robb and I stopped to see Old George. I wanted to thank him for helping you three children find your way out of the mountains —and I wanted to tell him about the gold on his land.

"It seems Old George has been reading that New Testament you gave him," Uncle Jack paused, "and it also seems that you children made quite an impression on the old man. He didn't want to let himself like you, but you children reminded him of his own boy who ran away from home when he was ten years old.

"After the son finished college and became a school teacher, he came back to ask his father's forgiveness. But Old George made up his mind he would never forgive his boy for running away from home. He said the boy was weak and timid and could never survive in the woods and that he was just a coward anyway."

"So the son," Robb took up the story, "came back to work in the woods to prove to his father that he was no coward. He found a job with the forest service in a look-out near his father's cabin. But the work was hard for him and he really was afraid of the forest. . . ."

"George Olson!" Ann understood with a gasp. "Is he Old George's son?"

"That's right," Uncle Jack smiled, "and all summer he has been trying to prove himself to his father—to win back his father's affection. When we told Old George about the gold, he was happy, but he was happiest of all because he has decided to be reconciled with his son. He said he read something about 'forgiveness' in that Bible you left him."

"Wow!" Ann exclaimed. "What a day of surprises. You don't have any more surprises, do you, Uncle Jack?"

"Well—just one more," the ranger's face was thoughtful. "When you children were lost, Aunt Betty and I prayed. It's been a long time since we prayed, but," he hesitated, "your aunt and I have been talking it over. We think next Sunday we will go along with you to the Chapel in the Pines."